To Giorgio, who's as quick as lightning, but always waits for me to catch up

First published in the United States, Canada, Australia, and New Zealand
in 2004 by North-South Books, an imprint of Nord-Süd Verlag AG,
Gossau Zürich, Switzerland.
Distributed in the United States by North-South Books Inc., New York.
Library of Congress Cataloging-in-Publication Data is available.
ISBN 0-7358-1917-3 (trade edition)
1 2 3 4 5 6 7 8 9 10
ISBN 0-7358-1918-1 (library edition)
1 2 3 4 5 6 7 8 9 10
Printed in Italy

Eva Montanari

Dino Bikes

Translated by J. Alison James

A Michael Neugebauer Book
North-South Books / New York / London

In an odd house on Dinosaur Hill a little dinosaur lived with his mother.
His name was Stego Saurus.

Every day Stego looked out of his window and watched the other young dinosaurs on their bikes.

They were as fast as lightning. They did tricks, laughing and calling to one another. They stopped with a screech of brakes.

Stego sighed. "If only I had a bike," he said sadly.

"You are so small," Mama Saurus said. "What if you fell and hurt yourself? You have to have good balance to ride a bike."

"I'll be careful," Stego promised. "I won't try any tricks."

At last his mother agreed.

"It is a special bike," his mother said. "It has four wheels. Two to ride on, and two to help you keep your balance. You can ride with all four wheels until you can keep your balance on your own."

Stego took off. He rode straight. He rode in a circle. He pushed the pedals back and the bike stopped. He could do it! It was easy! Waving to his mother, he zoomed off to join the others.

The other young dinosaurs raced around, their tails outstretched.
Stego felt shy. He biked up to join them, wobbling only a little.
"Hello," said Stego.

"Ho, ho! Who have we here?" called Croco, whose long mouth gleamed
in a continual grin. "Let's see that bike of yours."
The other dinosaurs came over and inspected Stego from all sides.
"He's just a kid," Tricera said.
"How many wheels does he need? One...two...I think I count four!"
Tyrono laughed rudely from his super-tall unicycle. "All I need is one,
and he can't even manage two?"
Stego wished the ground would open up and swallow him.

Then he had an idea. He jumped off his bike and removed the two little training wheels. Croco helped him, grinning all the while.
Now I'll have a real bike, Stego thought, just like the bigger dinosaurs.

But there was a problem. Riding a bike with just two wheels was a very wobbly experience. Stego kept the bike upright for a short, sweet second. Then he lost his balance. He teetered, he tottered, and he tumbled to the ground.

Stego heard mean laughter. It was Tyrono. "Go home, baby. You are too little to ride bikes with us!"
Stego looked and saw Tyrono high up on his unicycle, his cheeks puffed up with pride.
A tiny tear rolled down Stego's face and fell to the ground. Then another, and another.

Boom! Boom! Boom!

Could his little tears be that loud? No!
Dinosaur Hill was shaking! It wobbled
and wavered, then dropped with an even
louder *boom!* All the young dinosaurs tumbled
off their bikes and fell on top of each other
in a tangled mess on the heaving hill.

The hill was the neck of Bronto! Bronto the gigantic dinosaur had lost
his balance and fallen. His new bike lay beneath him. Two small wheels
rolled away.
All the young dinosaurs who had been riding up and down the hill looked
anxiously over the edge of Bronto's neck.

"What happened?" Stego asked Bronto.
Bronto bellowed, "You with all your talk
about riding with just two wheels!" He
shook his head, and all the dinosaurs fell
down again.
"As long as I can remember, I've wished for
a bike. Just because I was the littlest in my
family, my mother was afraid I'd get hurt.
Finally this morning, I got a bike. One with
training wheels! I started riding right away.
Then I listened to you and tried to go without
the training wheels. And *boom!*—I fell down."

Stego laughed with relief. This gigantic dinosaur, Bronto,
used training wheels too!
"I'll put mine back on if you do," Stego called out.
"It's a deal!" cried Bronto.

Bronto and Stego put on their training wheels again, and off they flew, dinosaurs biking on top of dinosaurs, balancing beautifully.